MARVEL
SUPER HERO
ADVENTURES

Meet Ant-Man
and the Wasp

Adapted by **Alexandra West**

Illustrated by **Dario Brizuela**

Based on the Marvel comic book characters **Ant-Man** and **the Wasp**

MARVEL
**Los Angeles
New York**

MarvelHQ.com

© 2018 MARVEL

SUSTAINABLE FORESTRY INITIATIVE
Certified Sourcing
www.sfiprogram.org
SFI-01415

Printed in the United States of America
First Edition, June 2018 10 9 8 7 6 5 4 3 2 1
Library of Congress Control Number: 2017955299
FAC-029261-18110
ISBN 978-1-368-02354-2

This is Scott Lang.

Scott is Ant-Man.

Ant-Man is a Super Hero!

This is Hope van Dyne.

Hope is the Wasp.

Wasp is a Super Hero!

Together, Scott and Hope
are Ant-Man and the Wasp.

Hope has a father.
His name is Hank Pym.
He is a scientist.

He creates the Ant-Man suit.
He creates the Wasp suit.

Hank gives Scott the
Ant-Man suit.

Hank gives Hope
the Wasp suit.

Ant-Man and
Wasp are a team.

They work together.
They each have
special powers.

Ant-Man can shrink!

Ant-Man can be as small as an ant.

Wasp can shrink, too!

Wasp can be as
small as a wasp.

Ant-Man can talk to ants.

He can ride them, too.

Ants help Ant-Man.

Wasp has wings.

They help her fly fast.

Her wings are strong.

Ant-Man can grow.

He becomes Giant-Man!

Giant-Man can grow
bigger than a building.

Wasp can fire blasts.
They come from her hands.

They are called
her Wasp Stings!

Ant-Man and Wasp use
their powers for good.

They fight Super Villains.

Ant-Man and Wasp
join the Avengers.

Ant-Man and Wasp
are tiny heroes.

Ant-Man and Wasp
are mighty heroes!